THE LOST
WORLD

CARNIVORA
THE WINGED
SCAVENGER

With special thanks to Cherith Baldry

To Elliot

www.beastquest.co.uk

ORCHARD BOOKS
338 Euston Road, London NW1 3BH
Orchard Books Australia
Level 17/207 Kent St, Sydney, NSW 2000

A Paperback Original
First published in Great Britain in 2010

Beast Quest is a registered trademark of Beast Quest Limited
Series created by Working Partners Limited, London

Text © Beast Quest Limited 2010
Cover and inside illustrations by Steve Sims © Orchard Books 2010

A CIP catalogue record for this book is available from
the British Library.

ISBN 978 1 40830 734 2

Printed and bound in China by Imago

The paper and board used in this paperback are natural recyclable
products made from wood grown in sustainable forests. The
manufacturing processes conform to the environmental regulations of
the country of origin.

Orchard Books is a division of Hachette Children's Books,
an Hachette UK company

www.hachette.co.uk

CARNIVORA
THE WINGED
SCAVENGER

BY ADAM BLADE

ORCHARD BOOKS

THE FOREST OF DOOM

SOUTHERN RIVER

THE SCARLET DESERT

Welcome to another world, where Dark Forces are at play.

Tom thought he was on his way back home; he was wrong. My son has entered another realm where nothing is as it seems. Six monstrous Beasts threaten all corners of the kingdom, and Tom and Elenna must face an enemy they thought long gone. I have never been so proud of my son, but can he be all that I always hoped he would be? Or shall a mother watch her son fail?

One question remains. Are you brave enough to join Tom on the most deadly Quest yet?

Only you know the answer...

Freya, Mistress of the Beasts

PROLOGUE

Tobias narrowed his eyes against the
icy wind as he trudged across the
Frozen Fields of Tavania towards his
ice lodge.

Behind him, he dragged the sack of
fish he'd just caught. The rope cut
into his hands, even through his
thick leather mittens.

It was a good catch, he thought. *If
I can sell all the fish in the market, I'll
have enough money to last me through
this dreadful season.*

Pausing to rest, Tobias looked up at the domed sky of Tavania. He was sure it was hanging lower than it once did. Worse than that, a dark rip stretched across it, from above his head almost to the horizon. Its edges looked like tattered shreds of cloud, and beyond them was a menacing dark portal.

Tobias couldn't imagine where it might lead.

"It gives me the creeps," he muttered. "And I'm not the only one, either."

The last time he had visited the market, all talk had been of the dreadful split in the sky.

"Is this the end of Tavania?" people were asking each other.

Tobias shook his head. There's no point in upsetting myself, he thought. He knew that Tavania had seen hard times before, and no doubt there would be hard times again. But his people had always been survivors.

A yap sounded from across the icefield as Karwai, Tobias's pet Arctic fox, bounded towards him. He pressed up against Tobias's legs as if he sensed his master's dark mood.

Tobias clumsily ruffled the fur on Karwai's head as he trudged on again, heaving at the heavy bag of fish.

He had only taken a couple of steps when Karwai's yaps changed to fierce growls, his gaze fixed on something up ahead.

Peering across the glimmering ice, Tobias made out several small shapes circling around him. As they drew closer he recognised them; they were young hyenas, their yellow-brown fur standing out clearly against the white wastes. *They're after my fish – but they're not getting it.*

"Here, you!" Tobias exclaimed. "Clear off!"

He stooped and grabbed a rock, which he hurled towards the circling cubs. They let out yelps of alarm and scampered a safe distance away, then wheeled round to face Tobias.

A moment later he spotted them again, slinking stealthily after him. Pity swept over him. They must be desperate. Hyenas don't usually come this far north.

He pressed on, trying to speed up. He had just spotted the roof of his ice lodge ahead of him when he felt a fierce tug at his shoulder. Karwai let out another growl. Tobias spun round to see the hyena cubs jumping onto his sack, trying to tear it apart with their tiny teeth.

"Hey, stop that!" he shouted.

He shook the rope angrily, trying to force the cubs to let go. But they were surprisingly strong, clinging to the sack with needle-sharp teeth and claws.

Karwai snarled at the cubs as Tobias pulled the sack closer towards him.

When he could lift it, he used all his strength to swing it round. He staggered, growing dizzy, as the cubs lost their grip and were flung off in all directions. They landed in the snow with high-pitched yelps of fury.

"Come on, Karwai! Chase them off!" Tobias called.

But instead of leaping after the hyena cubs, the Arctic fox froze at the sound of a low, mournful howling on the air.

"Karwai, what—" Tobias broke off as a blast of heat rolled across his back.

It scorched his thick fur coat and the back of his neck. With a yell of pain, Tobias fell in the snow. He rolled over to cool the heat on his

back. His eyes stretched wide as he looked up at the most hideous creature he had ever seen.

A giant hyena hovered above him. Its eyes were yellow as pus.

It circled menacingly above Tobias on broad wings jutting from its muscular shoulders.

Drawing spiny teeth back in a snarl, it lunged at Tobias and breathed a foul gust of air into his face. He gagged at the putrid stench. The air grew misty as the creature's breath swirled, sparks springing up inside the cloud. The fiery mist hovered in front of him, then faded.

Scrambling backwards, Tobias managed to struggle to his feet.

"Run, Karwai!" he yelled as he fled towards the lake.

Behind him he heard the excited grunts of the young hyenas as they chased him through the snow.

They must be that monster's young, he thought in a panic. *What am I going to do?*

His feet skidded on ice as he ran out onto the frozen surface of the lake, but he managed to keep his balance. Darkness swept over him as the monster's shadow covered him.

The hyena swooped down upon Tobias, and the air grew misty again, filled with thousands of tiny sparks.

Too late, Tobias heard the ice underfoot begin to crumble under the wave of heat. Jagged cracks ran across the surface; Tobias slipped as the ice tilted beneath him. With a yell of terror he plunged into the freezing water of the lake.

Cold stabbed him like the points of a million swords. Flailing in confusion, he turned over and over.

I'll die here, he thought as he choked on the icy water. *And no one will ever find my body...*

CHAPTER ONE

JOURNEY THROUGH THE ICE

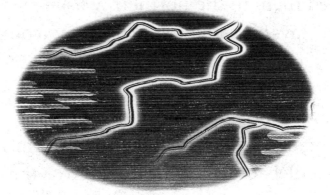

Tom shivered, blowing on his hands and rubbing them together. "I don't think I've ever been so cold!" he exclaimed.

"I know," Elenna replied, stamping her feet on the frozen ground. She shielded her face from the vicious, freezing wind that swept across the plain. "I can't feel my toes."

Three days and nights had passed since Tom and Elenna had sent Ellik home through the portal in the Misty Jungle. Now their Beast Quest had led them to the northern wastelands of Tavania – the last place they would visit in this kingdom to conquer a final Beast.

As they stopped to rest and share some bread and cheese from Storm's saddlebag, Tom gazed out across the icy terrain ahead. Snow stung his cheeks and he screwed up his eyes against the freezing blast.

"The north of Avantia is just as cold as this," Tom said, trying to forget how tired he felt.

Elenna nodded. "It's going to get colder, the further north we go."

"Well, we can't turn back," Tom said decisively. He delved into

Storm's saddlebag and took out the golden map that had appeared there at the beginning of his Beast Quest in Tavania. He'd already liberated five Beasts and sent them back to their rightful places. But there was one left to face. Was he ready for this final challenge?

Tom unfolded the golden panels of the map to reveal the jewelled mosaic inside. The glittering pieces of jade, crystal and quartz shifted as he gazed at them, and a glowing amber path led down from the mountains and across a plain. Shining words, The Frozen Fields, appeared across the flat expanse.

"That must be where we'll find the Beast," Elenna said, peering over Tom's shoulder.

"There's a lake, too," Tom added.

"The path is leading towards it. That's the way we have to go."

"I just wish I had a lovely warm fur coat like Silver!" Elenna said, shivering. "We could die of cold out here."

The grey wolf gave a sympathetic yelp, while Tom's black stallion, Storm, snorted out a long breath and shook his bridle.

"We'll be warmer when we're moving," Tom said, giving Storm's glossy neck a pat. "And I promise we'll find some warmer clothes as soon as we can. Surely someone will be in need of a few gold coins."

When Elenna had wrapped up the remains of their meal and stowed the bundle away in the saddlebag, Tom put away the map and mounted Storm.

Elenna scrambled up behind him.
With Silver padding alongside, they
set off through the bleak landscape.

Their path led them through the
foothills of the Rocky Mountains
and down onto the Frozen Fields.
The track they had been following
disappeared under a flat, white
blanket of snow that covered
everything.

"There's nothing to show us where
we're supposed to go," Tom said. He
cast a glance up at the sky. "And look
how dark it's getting!" The whole
dome of the sky was black, as if night
was falling, or a massive storm was
about to break. "I don't understand
it," Tom continued. "Tavania isn't like
Kayonia, where the days were short."

"Maybe we've been travelling so
long that we've lost track of time,"

Elenna suggested.

A crackle of lightning fizzed across the horizon. Tom suddenly realised what was making everything so dark.

"That's not nightfall – it's a portal!" he exclaimed.

Elenna clutched at him. "I've never seen one as big as that! It's covering the whole sky."

"I feel as though it's my fault," Tom went on, as he stared upwards.

"My coming here tore open these portals, and then Malvel used them to drag Beasts from their rightful homes and sent them where they don't belong."

"That's ridiculous!" Elenna protested. "Without you, there would be no hope for Tavania under Malvel's rule. You're about to face the very last Beast and send it home."

Tom was grateful, but he felt a swell of fear in his chest as he gazed at the rip above his head. It stretched from horizon to horizon, and beyond its ragged edges was black nothingness.

"Who knows what damage that could do to Tavania?" he murmured.

More determined than ever to find the Beast quickly, Tom urged Storm into a trot, with Silver loping alongside. Nothing could be seen on the flat plain except for a snow-covered hump; as they drew closer Tom realised it was a small ice-hut.

"Who would live out here?" Elenna asked in surprise.

"I don't know," Tom replied, "but we might be able to barter with them for furs." He guided Storm over to the hut and dismounted; Elenna slid down after him. As they approached the door, Storm began trotting in circles, and Silver bounded after him.

"That's right, boy!" Tom laughed. "That way you'll keep warm!"

Tom walked up to the door and knocked, but there was no answer. Exchanging a glance with Elenna, he knocked again, but there was still no response from inside the hut.

"There's no one here," Elenna said, disappointed.

Tom gave the door a push, and to his surprise it swung open. He stepped inside, glancing round warily.

"Hello?" he called. "Is anyone at home?"

The hut was a single small room. Footprints covered the floor, but a layer of dust over them showed that the hut's owner hadn't been there for some time. Bundles of furs and dried fish were hanging from the ceiling. The only furniture was a bed covered with furs, a small table, and a couple of rickety stools. Thrown across the stools were two long fur coats.

"That's exactly what we need," Elenna pointed out as she followed Tom into the hut. "But we can't just take them, can we?"

"I don't like it, but I think we have to," Tom replied. "If we freeze to death out here there'll be no one to defeat the Beast. Malvel will have won."

Elenna nodded. "You're right. We can leave some of the gold coins we brought from Gwildor."

Tom pulled out some of the coins and set them down on the table. Then he and Elenna each put on one of the coats. The bottoms brushed the floor, and the long sleeves covered their hands, so they had to roll them back.

As Tom pulled the heavy folds around him his hand slipped into a pocket, and his fingers closed round a leather pouch. Pulling it out, he saw that it was an empty glasses case.

"It's lovely and warm!" Elenna

exclaimed, wrapping the fur tightly
around herself. "I feel better already."

As he turned to leave, Tom spotted
a fishing spear leaning against the
wall. It was rusty, but when he felt
the point, it was sharp.

"I'll take this, too," he said, hooking

it over one shoulder by its leather strap. "It may come in useful later."

"Just in case," Elenna agreed.

Tom and Elenna stepped outside the hut again and closed the door behind them. The biting cold nipped at their noses, and their breath made clouds in the freezing air, but the furs protected them. Tom felt more confident as he called to Storm.

"This is the end of the Quest," he remarked. "We've one more Beast to find, and then we can attack the castle. Malvel had better watch out!"

Elenna headed away from the hut to meet Silver, who was bounding towards her. Suddenly she stopped.

"Tom, come and look at this!" she exclaimed.

When Tom joined her he saw a set of wide, deep pawprints in the snow, as if a large animal had passed by. On either side of the track were rows of smaller marks.

"What sort of creature could have made that?" Elenna asked. "We've never seen anything like it on a Quest before. It's got so many feet, and they're not all the same size!"

"It must be the Beast," Tom replied, stooping down to examine the marks as Silver padded up to give them a suspicious sniff. "We'll have to be on our guard – and smart."

He straightened up and gazed out across the empty snowfield. "Who knows what's out there?"

CHAPTER TWO

THE FROZEN LAKE

Tom and Elenna mounted Storm
again and set out to follow the tracks
through the snow.

Tom glanced around, ready for
Malvel's men to appear and attack
them. But nothing stirred in all the
icy wasteland.

Silver plodded alongside, keeping
well away from the paw prints of
the Beast.

A strong wind sent up flurries of snow.

Even though he could see nothing, Tom felt his heart beginning to pound. He knew that danger was near.

"I hope Jude managed to find Freya," he said, remembering the soldier's son. He'd helped them escape from the soldiers who had captured them during their Quest against Ellik.

"I'm sure he did," Elenna replied. "And I'm sure Freya will have gathered her rebel forces to challenge Malvel."

"Malvel has been gathering his army, too," Tom pointed out.

"And Freya will deal with them! One last battle, and Tavania will be free," Elenna said.

Tom nodded, feeling suddenly warmer at the thought of his mother's courage.

"Once we defeat this final Beast, we can join her," he said. "We'll get rid of Malvel and bring peace back to Tavania. And then – who knows? Perhaps we can go home."

Elenna's face flushed with pleasure at the thought of returning to her beloved Avantia.

The path had been gradually sloping up to the top of a shallow rise.

Beyond it, Tom saw a flat expanse of ice stretching in front of them.

"There's the frozen lake the map showed us," he said. "But where—"

"Tom!" Elenna interrupted. "Look at the footprints!"

Tom looked down from Storm's
back to the trail they had been
following. The deep prints in the
middle had come to an abrupt stop.
Only the smaller prints carried on
towards the lake.

"That's why the tracks look so strange!" Tom exclaimed. "There must be more than one Beast." He gave a confused glance over his shoulder at Elenna. "What on earth can they be?"

Elenna shook her head, just as bewildered. "And where are they?"

As he guided Storm down towards the frozen lake, Tom could see in every direction. But the landscape was empty.

"The Beast can't be far away," he said, his stomach churning. "Can it camouflage itself somehow?"

Tom shivered again: the cold was so bitter now that his eyelashes had frozen, and when he blinked tiny specks of ice got into his eyes.

When they reached the shore of the lake, Tom pulled out the map again. The jewelled squares shifted to show them the amber path leading out across the surface of the ice.

"We can't go across there!" Elenna objected. "What if the ice gives way?"

"But that's what the map tells us to do," Tom pointed out as he stowed it away again. "We have to risk it."

Elenna nodded reluctantly. They dismounted and led Storm cautiously out across the ice. Silver followed, his tail curled over his back and his head raised as he watched for any sign of movement. The small paw prints were harder to follow now; at first they caught glimpses where snow had sifted across the icy surface. Then they vanished altogether.

"Our final foe could be anywhere," Tom muttered.

Storm found it hard to set his

hooves down firmly on the slippery surface. Tom gripped his bridle to steady him; he and Elenna kept their eyes fixed on the ice, checking for any treacherous cracks.

Suddenly Elenna drew in a sharp breath. "Tom!" she choked out. "Look down – over here."

Tom glanced where she was pointing. Just beneath his feet he could see a human face, marked with what looked like burns on its cheeks and around its eyes. It floated just below the surface, bouncing against the underside of the ice. Its body melted into the dark shadows of the lake.

"He must have fallen in and drowned," Elenna said, her voice shaking. "How horrible!"

"Look at the marks on his face,"

Tom replied. "He didn't get those by
drowning. This must be the work of
the Beast."

Tom dragged his gaze away from
the dead man underneath the ice.

"I wonder if he's the owner of the
ice-hut we visited," he said with a
shiver. "Are we wearing his clothes?"

Peering down again, he could just make out a pair of glasses, hung round the dead man's neck on a piece of string. He felt a jolt like a blow to his stomach as he remembered the leather case he had found in the pocket of the coat he'd taken from the ice-hut.

I'm wearing a dead man's coat!

Tom fell to his knees and pounded on the frozen surface. But the ice was as thick as his thigh; he had to give up, letting out a grunt of frustration.

Elenna touched Tom's shoulder sympathetically. "There's nothing we can do to help him now," she murmured.

Tom scrambled to his feet again. "Then I'll find this Beast and defeat it," he promised. "Before it kills any more of Tavania's people."

He rummaged in Storm's saddlebag until he found the golden map and unfolded it again, attempting to locate the Beast. The mosaic showed the frozen lake and the glowing amber path they had taken to reach it, but there was no sign of the Beast.

Elenna let out a hiss. He looked up to see his friend rubbing her hands across her eyes.

"What's the matter?" he asked.

"The ice on my lashes has melted."

Tom put up a hand to touch his own lashes.

"Me too," he murmured, baffled.

He noticed that the air was a little warmer, even though they were in the middle of the frozen lake.

"I don't understand this," he said. "How can it be getting warmer?"

Elenna stared around, sniffing.

"There's a strange smell in the air," she said. "Like something rotting…"

A low-pitched, guttural howl sounded on the air. A shiver ran down Tom's spine as the sound echoed across the wastes of ice.

"That must be the voice of the Beast!" he whispered.

CHAPTER THREE

THE FINAL PORTAL

Silver launched himself towards the
terrifying sound, his paws slipping
and sliding on the ice.

"No, Silver! Stop!" Elenna cried.

Tom and Elenna tried to run after
the wolf, but they couldn't leave
Storm behind, and the stallion's
hooves slipped as he struggled to
trot across the surface of the lake.

"Stop, Silver!" Tom yelled as the

wolf pelted on into the distance.

Silver took no notice. Tom called him again, but broke off as his feet slipped. He felt the sudden weightlessness of a fall, and braced himself to crash down on the ice.

Then Tom caught sight of his shadow on the ice below. It hung there, barely moving.

I'm...I'm floating!

Something invisible tugged at him, trying to drag him into the yawning hole in the sky.

He gasped as he saw that his feet had been lifted right off the frozen surface; his arms flapped as he tried to steady himself.

As Tom rose further he heard a startled cry from Elenna.

"You're floating, too!" Tom cried.

Clutching at each other, they

gradually sank down until their feet touched the ice again.

Tom saw that the fur of Elenna's coat was stretching up, as if trying to rise into the sky. As Tom's gaze rose he saw the dark rip, like jaws about to swallow them. The portal!

"That was close," Tom gasped. "The portal almost sucked us into it."

"Who knows where we would have ended up if we'd gone through it?" Elenna said, gazing up fearfully.

"But Storm's all right," Tom pointed out, shuffling over to the stallion while still keeping a grip on Elenna's arm. "It's because he's so much heavier. We'd better hang onto him."

He planted his feet more firmly on the ground, trying to sink his weight down to his feet.

"We'll have to watch every step from now on," Elenna said, as she grabbed Storm's bridle. "One false move and we could be dragged up into that abyss."

Tom looked around for Silver; he couldn't spot the grey wolf, but he could hear his mournful howling. Snow had begun to drift upwards into the portal and Tom's stomach

churned with fear as he wondered
if the wolf had been dragged up
there too.

"There he is!" Elenna exclaimed.

Tom made out the familiar shape of
Silver; he was sitting on the ice with
his head flung back as he howled
at the sky. The wolf obviously
understood that something was very
wrong. Tom felt the portal tugging
harder at him, and the smell of rot in
the air grew stronger.

"The Beast must be close," Tom
muttered. "But where is it?"

Suddenly, Silver's howls changed to
excited yelps as a horde of hyena
cubs charged out of the snowy haze.

"That must be what Silver was
running towards," Elenna said.

"Yes, but what are hyenas doing
so far north?" Tom asked.

"They can't live on the ice."

Still gripping Storm's bridle, Tom and Elenna set out towards the wolf and the horde of cubs. Silver bent his head, nudging the little creatures in an attempt to stop them hurting themselves. They bounced on the ice like furry balls, as if the portal was pulling at them.

"These little cubs never made the howling noise we heard," he told Elenna. "Their mother must be somewhere close by..."

Her voice died away as Silver flinched in pain. At first Tom couldn't see what the matter was. Then, as he looked closer, he spotted spurts of flame coming from the cubs' jaws.

"Hey – the cubs are breathing fire at Silver!" he exclaimed.

The hyena cubs shot jets of flame

from their mouths, singeing Silver's
fur. The wolf started back with a yelp
of pain and shock.

"No! Get off!" Elenna yelled angrily.

Tom stared at the young hyenas. He
drew his sword and heard Elenna
unhooking her crossbow, ready to
go to the wolf's help.

But before either of them could
attack, a foul stench of air hit Tom
in the face. The snowy mist rising
towards the portal parted to reveal a
huge Beast flying towards him. Tom
gazed at the massive hyena with
wings and yellow eyes that seemed to
drip poison. Powerful hooked claws
stretched out towards Tom, and her
jaws parted to reveal huge teeth.

She let out a jet of hot air that
burst into flames; Tom ducked his
head to avoid the stinging darts of

heat. This must be how the dead man under the ice got burned!

Tom was aware that the red jewel in his belt had started to glow – the jewel that he had won in Gorgonia that helped him to understand the thoughts of Beasts. The name Carnivora throbbed in his mind.
So that's who you are, he thought.

The hyena plunged towards Tom, her claws extended. Still clinging to Storm's bridle with one hand, Tom gripped his sword in the other and swung it in a mighty stroke.

A jolt ran up his arm as his blade made contact. But instead of cutting through the wing, the blade shattered into pieces, as if it was made of glass.

No! The metal must have got too cold. And how strong is this Beast, to withstand a steel blade!

Tom dropped the useless sword hilt and raised his shield. Fire had charred it, but it was the only protection he had. He struggled to unhook the fish spear from his shoulder, but it was tangled in the thick fur of his coat.

No...he thought as Carnivora wheeled round and swooped down for another attack. Is this how our last Quest ends?

CHAPTER FOUR

BATTLE AGAINST THE BEAST

Elenna let go Storm's bridle to load her crossbow; bolts zipped through the air as she fired at the Beast. But Carnivora swatted them aside with her wings. Elenna went on shooting, only to let out a cry of frustration as her last bolt bounced harmlessly off the Beast's body.

Carnivora let out a howl of rage;

there was a frenzied glare in her pus-filled eyes. She doesn't belong here, Tom knew. The cold is driving her mad. She swept past, kicking out at Storm as she flew above him.

The stallion threw up his head and let out a startled whinny, pulling his bridle away from Tom. Tom stumbled as he lost his grip, and felt the portal tugging at him.

Storm galloped aside as Carnivora turned to dive down on him again. Tom heard an ominous crack and saw jagged lines fanning out from beneath the stallion's hooves.

"No! The ice is breaking up!" Elenna cried.

Storm had halted, shaking his mane. Elenna headed towards him, but Tom grabbed her arm.

"That won't help," he told her as

she struggled with him. "The ice around him is already weakened. If we add any more weight, we could all fall through."

Elenna stopped struggling and nodded reluctantly. "Come on, Storm," she said, holding out a hand in an effort to coax the horse back onto the firmer ice.

Anger surged through Tom as he watched the winged hyena circling menacingly overhead. He reached once again for the fishing spear he had taken from the ice hut.

Unhooking it from his shoulder, he flung the spear at Carnivora, but it fell short and clanged down onto the ice.

Tom scrambled to pick it up and lunged at the Beast as she homed in on him. The Beast lashed out with a wing and Tom had to duck to avoid being knocked from his feet. He could still feel the tug of the portal; he had to concentrate on keeping his feet firmly on the ground.

Carnivora let out another blast of hot air that burst into flames as it bore down on Tom. The Beast let out more jets of hot air that flared up, throwing off burning sparks as they swirled around Tom's head. He felt the sparks singe his eyebrows and the flames licking over his skin.

As Tom stumbled backwards to escape the fire, his feet slipped and he stabbed the spear point into the icy surface of the lake to stop himself from falling. The blow wasn't hard enough to break through, but it threw up chunks of ice that scattered around his feet.

Elenna had just persuaded Storm to step gingerly back onto the stronger part of the surface. She turned, staring at the scraps of shattered ice.

Then, to Tom's surprise, she dropped to the ground beside Storm and grabbed up one of her fallen

crossbow bolts. She began jabbing it
into the ice, scooping up long shards.

"What are you doing?" Tom asked.
He raised his spear, ready to hurl it at
Carnivora. "Why are you scrabbling
about in the ice?"

"Just watch," Elenna replied. Rising
to her feet, she fitted one of the long
splinters of ice into her crossbow.

Carnivora swooped down again;
Elenna held up the crossbow, her
eyes narrowed. As soon as the Beast
opened her jaws to breathe out heat
again, Elenna fired her makeshift
ice dart.

The dart hit the jet of air as it left
Carnivora's mouth. The blast of hot
air shattered the shard of ice into

hundreds of deadly, needle-sharp splinters that punctured the Beast's skin and embedded themselves in her flesh.

The winged hyena let out a howl of pain and confusion. Clawing at her own fur, she spun uncontrollably in the air.

Tom felt a thrill of exhilaration. "Great thinking, Elenna!" Crouching down, he stabbed the spear point over and over again into the ice, and passed icicle after icicle to Elenna. When he managed to split off a bigger shard, he used it as a second spear, flinging it at the enraged Beast.

Elenna fired with pinpoint accuracy, giving Carnivora no chance to renew her attack. More and more icy splinters buried themselves in her flesh. The Beast flapped her wings frantically to gain height, hovering closer and closer to the portal.

The pull of the portal was growing stronger. Tom felt it lift him clear of the ice. Elenna's feet were leaving the ground, too. He grabbed at her to keep them both from flying up into the air.

Suddenly, a burst of frightened howling broke out. Tom's gaze was dragged over to where Silver and the hyena cubs were lifted right into the air, powerless to resist the powerful tugging from the sky.

We need to defeat this Beast quickly! Tom realised. *Otherwise, we'll be dragged to our deaths above the clouds.*

CHAPTER FIVE

MANY FRIENDS

"Silver! No!" Tom skidded forward, sliding along on his knees as he clutched at Silver.

He grabbed the wolf's tail as he was carried into the air. Dragging him over to Storm, he fastened the stallion's reins around Silver's paw. The grey wolf let out a whimper of protest.

"Don't worry, boy," Tom reassured

him. "You'll be safe there, and it won't be for long." *I hope that's true*, he thought.

Meanwhile the struggling hyena cubs were whirled into the air, scrabbling furiously and whining. They sent out desperate jets of fire from their jaws, and started to bite and claw at each other as they climbed higher in the sky. Tom could hardly bear to watch.

"Those poor things," Elenna murmured. "They're terrified."

Finally, they were sucked up into the portal, disappearing to wherever it led. Carnivora howled in distress as she saw them go, momentarily forgetting her fight. Then, with a snap of jaws, she swivelled back round, fury lighting her eyes. She wanted revenge and the only people around were Tom and his friend.

"We need to end this," Tom said.

"I know," said Elenna, fitting another icicle to her bow.

She aimed at the Beast's left wing. Her bolt hit it squarely in the middle and the Beast cried out with pain, her putrid breath making Tom gag.

Carnivora spun out of control; her wings flapped wildly as she plummeted to the ground, hitting the ice with a thump. At once Tom thrust out his legs; using his spear to propel himself, he slid across the ice to the Beast's side. Scrambling up onto her chest, he held the point of his spear to her neck. Carnivora glared at him as he held her at his mercy.

"I could kill you now," he said, though he had no idea if the Beast would understand.

But the portal was still pulling at
them. Tom leapt down and Carnivora
half lifted from the ground. Suddenly,
the Beast rose into the air, faster and
faster as she drew closer to the portal.
She tore through low clouds,
speeding up towards the ugly black
slash in the sky. At last she was
carried through it, and the rip in the
sky closed.

"She's gone!" Elenna exclaimed.

"I hope she's back in her own home, and that she finds her cubs again."

"The portal has gone, too," Tom added, with a huge sigh of relief. It was good to feel his feet firmly on the ground again as the terrible pull vanished. "And that's the last of them. Tavania is safe."

So why don't I feel happier? Tom wondered.

The air shimmered. Mist swirled round Tom and Elenna; when it faded they found themselves on the edge of a wood. Through the outermost trees they could see the walls of the capital city and the castle where Malvel's black flag still flew from the topmost tower.

"We've left the ice behind!" Elenna said, slipping off her fur coat and draping it over the branch of a tree.

Tom felt himself beginning to sweat in the heavy furs. The air was so much warmer here, after the bitter cold of the Frozen Fields. He stripped off his coat, too, and hung it beside Elenna's.

Storm trotted up beside Tom, while Silver bounded over to Elenna. Both their animal friends looked calm and healthy. Tom realised that the pain from the burns Carnivora had given him had vanished completely.

"How did we get here?" Elenna asked, looking round in wonder as she ruffled Silver's grey fur.

Before Tom could reply, the wizard Oradu appeared in front of him. Tom's eyes widened as he realised that this wasn't a vision; the real Oradu was standing there. The Good Wizard wore his robe and hat, and held his staff in one hand. His cauldron was by his side, and his pet falcon perched on his shoulder.

With the other hand, Oradu held out a thick book bound in leather with mystical symbols on the cover. "Now I have my spellbook back," he said, smiling. "The last thing Malvel took from me. My magic is as strong as ever it was. And it's all thanks to you, Tom, and you, Elenna."

Tom felt a bolt of energy rush through him as he gazed at Oradu.

"Tavania must be safe, now that you're back to challenge Malvel!" he exclaimed.

"Almost. There's no time to waste," Oradu said. "I brought you here into the woods to be reunited with Tavania's heroes, and reclaim the city. Follow me, but be careful.

Malvel's men might be lurking."

The wizard led the way deeper into the woods. They had not walked far when Tom began to hear the sound of voices coming from somewhere ahead. The undergrowth rustled and twigs snapped under the tread of feet.

Tom felt his nerves stretched tight, wondering if Malvel's soldiers were heading their way.

A few moments later he and Elenna were surrounded by armed men and women. But these were not Malvel's grim soldiers, in their black armour. They wore no uniform; instead of steel mail they were dressed in leather jerkins, and they were armed with scythes and fishing spears as well as swords and bows.

Among them, Tom spotted King Henri, carrying a sword with a ruby in its hilt. He didn't meet Tom's gaze, looking ashamed that he had lost control of his kingdom.

"This is the rebel army Freya has gathered together," Oradu said.

The soldiers crowded round Tom and Elenna, trying to shake their hands and calling out greetings.

"Welcome back!"

"You've conquered the last Beast!"

One of the men, his eyes shining with delight, pointed to the sky. "Look – no more portals!"

"Tavania owes you thanks!"

Struggling to move through the heaving crowd, Tom spotted a familiar face. "Look, Elenna," he pointed. "There's Jude!"

"He looks pleased to see us," Elenna said, giving the boy a wave.

Though all the warriors were

smiling, Tom could see the steel in their eyes. They were ready to fight for Tavania's freedom.

"Tom! Tom!"

He turned to see his mother, Freya, pushing her way through the crowd. Her armour gleamed. Reaching him, she folded him into a tight hug.

"It's good to see you again," she said happily.

Tom's heart swelled with joy to be reunited. "You too," he replied. "Is all well here?"

Freya's eyes shone as she gazed at her son. "Very well. I don't think you'll recognise Dalaton when you see him!"

"I think I will," Tom said with a grin. "I saw a vision of him. Tavania has a new Master of the Beasts now."

As he finished speaking, a tall man

came towards him, the soldiers falling
back to let him through. Dalaton was
dressed in shining armour, and he
bore himself proudly, like a warrior.

"It's thanks to your mother that
I found my destiny," he said.

Dalaton's paunch and slouched stance were gone; now his body was strong and muscled.

Two soldiers had followed Dalaton; now he called them forward. One of them was carrying Tom's sword and shield, while the other had Elenna's bow and her quiver of arrows.

They bowed as they presented the weapons to their owners.

"Recovering your weapons was my last task as a guard," Dalaton said.

"Thank you!" Tom exclaimed.

His body tingled with confidence as he slipped his shield onto his arm and gripped the hilt of his sword. Elenna's eyes were glowing as she slung the quiver over her shoulder and tested her bowstring.

"We have amassed thousands of rebels to attack the kingdom," Freya

went on, "hiding from Malvel in the forest caves. But Malvel's forces still outnumber us, and they're well-armed and protected by a fortress."

Tom stepped up to his mother's side. "We have honour and justice on our side," he announced to the watching crowd. He thrust his sword into the air. "We will win this final battle!"

CHAPTER SIX

ATTACK ON THE CASTLE

Freya divided the army into two separate squads; she would lead one herself, and Dalaton would command the other. Tom watched, proud of how calm his mother was.

"Elenna," she said, beckoning to Tom's friend, "I want you to lead the first wave of archers who will cover the soldiers as they attack."

Elenna's eyes widened in dismay. "I can't! I'm not good enough!"

"Of course you are." Tom gave her a friendly nudge. "There's no one better than you for the job."

"Tom's right," Freya said encouragingly. "I wouldn't have chosen you otherwise."

Elenna managed to smile, and Freya showed her where the archers were getting into position. Tom stood beside his mother and Oradu as Dalaton leapt up onto a tree stump to address the rebel army.

"A kingdom is not made by its ruler, but by its people," he began. "Tavania has been plunged into darkness by a corrupt king. But together we – the good people of Tavania – can bring back the light."

His gaze swept the ranks of soldiers,

warm with pride. "Today there are no farmers, no peasants, not even warriors," he continued. "Today, there are only kings. Today, each and every one of us is king of Tavania. Now, we reclaim our kingdom!"

The army burst into loud cheering, beating their swords against their shields. Tom cheered with them. He jumped onto Storm's back, ready to charge at Dalaton's command.

Tavania's new hero leapt down from the tree stump and came towards him. "Are you ready, Tom?" Dalaton asked.

"I never back down from any challenge," he told Dalaton, forcing his voice to sound strong and steady. "I'll be proud to fight alongside the people of Tavania."

Dalaton's smiled. "We're proud to

have you with us, Tom."

Tavania's Master of the Beasts mounted his own horse – a long-legged stallion – and rode to the head of his squad. He led them through the trees until they could see Malvel's castle across the valley.

"Are you ready, Malvel?" Tom muttered, gazing at the black flag that flew from the topmost tower. "Your reign ends today!"

Dalaton turned to look back at his soldiers one last time. "While our hearts beat, our spirits soar!" he cried. "Let them soar above evil and grind it into the ground!"

Facing the castle again, he spurred his horse into a trot. He raised his sword, and the sunlight flashed on it, turning the blade into dazzling white flame. "For Tavania!"

The rebel army took up the cry as they swept down the slope into the valley. The sound of their hoofbeats was like thunder.

Tom urged Storm forward, riding after Dalaton at the head of a group of swordsmen. "For Tavania!" he echoed, as the wind swept through his hair. "For Tavania!"

CHAPTER SEVEN

UNEXPECTED HELP

"For Tavania! For Tavania!"

The soldiers stormed through the city gates, the leading horses battering down the oaken barriers with their hooves. They galloped along the streets to charge at the palace walls. The townspeople leapt out of their way with cries of terror as they swept past. Exhilaration

drove out Tom's fear as he picked up
speed, using the magic of Tagus's
horseshoe, embedded in his shield.

*It feels so good to have my own weapons
back!* Tom thought.

Mounted on Storm, Tom rode at
the head of Dalaton's squad as they
headed for the main gate of the
palace. Freya was leading her troops
to attack from the rear. The streets
emptied as the last of the citizens
darted into their homes and slammed
the doors.

When the army reached the castle,
Tom could hear yells of shock coming
from inside the walls, but still no
soldiers appeared to challenge them.
Arrows flew overhead from Elenna's
team of archers, who bombarded the
defenders with shots arcing over
the walls.

"Bring the ram!" Dalaton cried.

Some of Dalaton's men dragged up a battering ram: a huge tree trunk tipped with an iron point, mounted on wheels. The soldiers took up positions on either side and thrust it over and over again at the palace gates.

"Keep going," Dalaton ordered. "It can't hold out much longer."

But though the gates shuddered under the blows, they held fast.

"Stand back!" The wizard Oradu's voice rang out. Then the air shimmered and the wizard appeared beside Tom and Dalaton.

Oradu stood in front of the gates, his feet apart to brace himself and his hands held out in front of him. He shouted a single word in a language Tom had never heard before.

Crimson fire blazed out from his hands; as it struck the door the heavy oaken planks exploded, scattering splinters everywhere. Tom and the Tavanian soldiers flung up their shields to block the flying debris.

Tom gasped with admiration as he

cked under the shower of splinters.
alvel's evil soldiers fled as the gate
was destroyed, and the way into the
palace lay open.

*This is why we fought so hard to give
Oradu his strength back. Now he can help
us in the final battle!*

With Dalaton at their head, the
army of rebels surged into the castle.

Now was the time to fight. Malvel's
soldiers swarmed forward, their
swords raised, as angry cries filled
the air.

Tom followed Dalaton closely,
swinging his sword at Malvel's men.
He slipped from Storm's saddle to
fight better and a soldier lunged at
him. Tom quickly raised his sword to
block the attack. His blade slid down
the other man's until they jammed at
the hilt.

They stared into each other's eyes. Tom could feel his arms trembling.

Then he called on the better fighting skills that came from the amber jewel in his belt. He twisted his sword to one side, sending the man falling to his knees.

Tom glanced up at one of the castle turrets. A dark face was glaring down at him from an upper window, its features twisted in fury. Malvel!

But Tom had no time to think about the wizard. Malvel's men were trying to force the rebels out of the castle courtyard. Tom struggled hard to find space to swing his sword in the crush. Swords clanged against swords; shields clattered against shields. Shouts of anger and the cries of the wounded filled the air as Tom fought his way towards the castle.

This is the only way Tavania can
be free!

Malvel's forces had recovered from
their first shock. A trumpet sounded
and the clanging of a bell split the air.
More enemy soldiers pounded out
of the castle from every direction,
beginning to force Dalaton's army
back towards the gateway.

Tom spotted Oradu; the good wizard was firing off spells, but they seemed to fade into the air without doing any damage. Tom couldn't understand it. He looked up in the direction Oradu was aiming, and saw Malvel in the turret window.

Small jets of light were flashing from the Evil Wizard's fingers. They met Oradu's spells in mid-air, and turned them into harmless sparks.

Tom climbed back into the saddle and manoeuvred Storm to stand next to Dalaton's horse. Dalaton suddenly let out a cry of joy and triumph.

He pointed behind Malvel's troops, to where Freya, at the head of her squad, was falling on the enemy from behind. Some of Malvel's men turned to face her, and Dalaton's squad began pushing forward.

Hope surged through Tom. His heart swelled with joy as he caught glimpses of his mother in the crowd, cutting down soldier after soldier with skilful sweeps of her blade.

Malvel's men were beginning to panic, caught between the two squads of the rebel army.

But we're still outnumbered, Tom thought. He knew that as soon as Malvel's men rallied, the balance would tip in their favour. What can we do? An idea surged through Tom.

"Dalaton!" he cried. "Call for the Beasts. They will return for you, as you are the Master of the Beasts! Call for them now, before it's too late!"

Understanding dawned on Dalaton's face. He raised his sword into the air. "Come, Beasts! Come save your kingdom!"

CHAPTER EIGHT

FACING MALVEL

"Yes!" Tom let out a shout of triumph.

The Beasts of Tavania appeared in the centre of the courtyard. Ellik was the first to land, her rainbow coloured body coiling on the ground. Her massive jaws gaped as she sent out a bolt of dazzling energy that scattered Malvel's men.

Madara followed, a streak of white

fur leaping down to pounce on a soldier who was about to plunge his sword into the boy, Jude. Her ebony claws sank into the terrified man as she dragged him to the ground.

Convol reared up on his hind legs and swept his clubbed tail from side to side, toppling the enemy soldiers with massive blows. Malvel's soldiers were stunned with shock and panic, running in all directions.

Krestor and Carnivora arrived side by side over the outer wall. Krestor stretched out his long neck, clubbing Malvel's soldiers with his head as he swooped down. Together he and Carnivora hovered above Hellion, whose rolling flames were heading for the castle wall, his eyes blazing in fury. Krestor's spines fired jet of acids into the air, which mingled with a

misty cloud of Carnivora's breath.

A fireball exploded over Hellion's head; the fiery Beast added its power to his own flames and barrelled through the wall of the castle.

Tom was still staring when he felt a hand grip his shoulder. He turned to see Dalaton.

"Tom," the new warrior began, "you must get into the castle and go after Malvel. If he can be overcome, his minions will fade away in defeat. That is what will bring light back to Tavania."

Tom nodded, full of pride that Dalaton should choose him for this mission. "Whatever happens now," he said, "it has been an honour to fight beside you."

"The honour was mine," Dalaton replied, smiling. "Now, go!"

Tom kicked his heels into Storm's flanks, guiding the stallion through the chaos in the courtyard as they raced for the gap in the palace wall. Two of Malvel's soldiers threw themselves into his way, but the power of Storm and the skill of Tom's sword scattered them aside.

As Storm picked his way through the ruins of the wall, Tom felt a pair of hands clutching at his legs. He looked down, ready to strike at another of the enemy soldiers.

Instead, he saw Elenna. She gave him a swift grin as she scrambled into the saddle behind him. Silver bounded at the stallion's heels.

"Somehow I feel this is going to be our last meeting with Malvel," Elenna said. "Nothing is going to make me miss it!"

Warmth enveloped Tom to have his friend with him. "Have you seen my mother?" he asked as he guided Storm up a spiral staircase just wide enough for the horse to pass.

He knew that if this palace was like the one in Avantia, this should be the way to the throne room.

"Don't worry," Elenna replied. "The way Freya was fighting, she could probably take on all Malvel's army by herself!"

The spiral staircase led to a landing; Tom saw the doors to the throne room in front of him. "Go, boy!" he shouted. He urged Storm forward, then tugged on the reins so that the stallion would rear up and batter down the doors with his front hooves. The crash echoed through the palace as the doors gave way.

Tom and Elenna dismounted and
guided Storm through the debris,
with Silver close behind. As he
entered the throne room, Tom
expected to see Malvel, and braced
himself for any evil spell the wizard
might launch at him.

Instead, Oradu stood in one corner of the room. His gaze was fixed on the floor, and he was muttering spells in a strange language.

Beyond the wizard, a shimmering green portal had replaced one wall of the throne room. A faint, foul air drifted through it; Tom felt sick as the smell wreathed round him.

Silver whined and growled at the wizard, the fur on his shoulders bristling. *What's the matter with him?* Tom wondered.

Elenna gripped Tom's shoulders. "What's happening?" she whispered.

Oradu looked up. "Malvel knew the game was up," he said, gesturing at the shimmering green curtain. "He has fled through the portal into Avantia. You can chase him if you like. Without Malvel's magic, his

soldiers here won't last much longer.
Dalaton and Freya can deal with
them easily."

Tom gazed at the wizard, frowning.
He didn't want to leave his mother
behind in Tavania, but he knew that
if he didn't pursue Malvel right away,
his arch enemy might escape into
Avantia.

*And who knows what damage he might
do there?* Tom thought. With an
uneasy glance at Elenna, he took a
step towards the portal.

Whoosh! A bolt of pure red light
blasted past his ear and struck Oradu
full in the chest. Elenna cried out in
dismay as the wizard fell to the floor
and lay there lifeless. Their friend
was dead!

CHAPTER NINE

THROUGH THE PORTAL

As Tom stood frozen in shock, a red aura rose from Oradu's body.

"What's happening?" Elenna exclaimed. "Is he losing his magic?"

A voice spoke from behind Tom. "Yes. His magic is leaving him."

Tom raised his sword and spun round. Then he froze. Standing in the doorway of the throne room was…Oradu! Smoke curled from his fingers.

Tom stared from one Oradu to the other. "What's going on?" he demanded.

The lifeless form on the floor began to shimmer and change. Its robes darkened, and its face grew thin and cruel.

"It's not Oradu – it's Malvel!" Elenna gasped. "Silver, you knew all the time," she added. "That's why you growled at him. Clever boy!"

"Malvel nearly tricked us," Tom said. Sheathing his sword, he added, "It's just as well we have a Good Wizard on our side."

A tingle of excitement passed through Tom as he realised that his old enemy Malvel had finally been drained of his magic. At last the evil wizard was at the mercy of good!

"Where does this portal lead?" he asked Oradu, pointing at the shimmering green veil.

Oradu strode forward and stood in front of the portal, examining it carefully. "I believe it is a mystical pathway into Gorgonia," he replied at last.

Fury flashed through Tom. "Of course!" he exclaimed. "Malvel would try to trick us into entering the Dark Realm, where he has ultimate power."

"He'd love to get his hands on us there," Elenna agreed.

Tavania's Good Wizard waved his hand over the portal, and the green colour turned to a deep sea-blue. The foul smell faded, replaced by a clean tang like an ocean breeze.

"There!" Oradu said with satisfaction. "Now the portal leads into Avantia."

The lifeless heap that was Malvel suddenly sprang to his feet. Knocking Elenna aside, he scrambled to reach the portal. Tom flung himself at the dark wizard and wrestled Malvel to the ground.

"Oh, no, you don't!" he muttered through gritted teeth. "You're not going into Avantia without us."

"Take your hands off me!" the wizard snarled.

Elenna leapt to Tom's aid and the two of them managed to wrestle Malvel through the portal. Silver bounded after them and Oradu gently guided Storm through.

Malvel kicked, punched and scratched. Even though he had lost

his magic, he was still strong. Tom
and Elenna together could scarcely
hold onto him.

"We have to go!" Tom called out to
Oradu. "Thank you for everything."

"It is Tavania who owes you
thanks," the Good Wizard replied.

Malvel was still struggling. Tom swung his shield round and knocked him dizzy. Then he drew his sword and held it at Malvel's neck. "Now be still!" he ordered.

Malvel snarled out a curse. "You'll regret this, boy," he threatened, but stopped fighting.

The tip of Tom's blade nicked his flesh, and a trickle of black blood ran down his neck.

"Don't even think of moving!" Tom snapped.

Behind Malvel, Tom could see that the portal was beginning to shrink.

There was a sudden commotion on the landing outside: hoarse shouting and the clash of swords.

Freya appeared in the doorway of the throne room, in the middle of a cluster of rebel soldiers. Her back was to Tom as Malvel's men thrust the rebels into the throne room; the battle had found its way right into the castle!

Tom's heart swelled with pride as he saw how Freya defended herself.

But the portal was shrinking, blotting out Tom's view of the throne room. He felt as though a curtain was closing over his mother, cutting her off from him.

"Mother!" he shouted. "Over here, be quick! You can still pass through the portal!"

But Freya did not hear him above the clanging of swords and the yells of wounded men.

"Mother!" Tom called again, his voice growing hoarse. *I can't lose her a second time, not so soon after I found her!* he thought.

Tom ignored Malvel's vindictive chuckle as he felt the portal begin to drag him away. His gaze was fixed on Freya, almost completely surrounded by the enemy.

"You must come now!" he begged.

Suddenly one of Malvel's soldiers broke away from the fight and dashed for the portal. "I will save my king!" he yelled.

Tom tensed, feeling a thrill of fear as the power of the portal dragged him away. He couldn't release his grip on Malvel to attack the soldier, and he wasn't sure he still had the strength to fight.

Before Tom could decide what to do, Silver bounded past him and leapt through the shrinking portal entrance. He blocked the soldier, sinking his teeth into the man's arm.

As Silver flung himself forward, the
soldier lost his balance and fell to
the floor, rolling further into the
throne room.

"No!" Elenna screamed.

The portal shrank to a dot and
closed for good. Silver was stranded
in Tavania.

CHAPTER TEN

HOME TO AVANTIA

Tom felt himself become weightless. The world around him twirled and shimmered in a rainbow of colours as the portal carried them away. He heard a nervous whinny from Storm, and a hiss of rage from Malvel.

Tom saw Elenna floating beside him as they rushed through the portal. Hardly any time seemed to pass before Tom saw King Hugo's castle appear at the other end of the tunnel of blue light. Still dragging Malvel, he hurried towards it and burst out into the castle courtyard. The evil wizard let out a snarl of fury as he realised where he was.

King Hugo and Wizard Aduro stood facing them; the Good Wizard had his hands extended, ready to cast a spell. The worried expressions on their faces changed to delight as they saw Tom and Elenna.

"It's you!" the wizard exclaimed, lowering his hands. "I was worried that evil was passing into Avantia."

"It has," Tom replied grimly. He thrust Malvel to his knees in front of King Hugo. "But now it is helpless. Malvel has lost his magic."

The king and Aduro looked down

at the Evil Wizard, shock and disgust on their faces.

Malvel spat contemptuously. "Weaklings! One day I will have my revenge," he threatened.

Tom ignored him. "Malvel will answer for his crimes against Avantia and Tavania," he said to the king.

King Hugo nodded, while Aduro muttered an incantation. With an angry yell, Malvel faded into a dark, wispy shape and then vanished.

"He's safely locked up in the castle dungeon," Aduro said.

"Tom! Tom!"

Tom spun round. His father was sprinting towards him across the courtyard.

"It's so good to see you!" Taladon exclaimed, gripping Tom by the shoulders. His eyes shone with joy and relief. "I lost touch with you after we left Kayonia. Even Aduro couldn't work out where you had gone."

King Hugo nodded gravely. "I had to send word to your aunt and uncle in Errinel that you might have been lost for ever. Now I can send them the good news that you and Elenna have returned unharmed. They will—"

King Hugo broke off, frowning. "But you aren't all here," he went on. "What happened to Freya and Marc and Silver?"

Tom swallowed. "Malvel took Marc's life," he said, his voice breaking. "And Freya and Silver couldn't make it to the portal. They're still in Tavania."

As he spoke, Elenna buried her face in her hands. Tom put an arm around her shoulders, but he knew it wasn't enough.

Taladon bowed his head in grief, but only for a moment. Then Avantia's Master of the Beasts collected himself, gazing at Tom. "Freya will look after Silver," he said firmly. "I know we will all be reunited one day. We must stay strong."

"Come to the castle," King Hugo invited. "You need to rest."

As they followed the king across the courtyard and through the castle door, Tom turned to Elenna. Her eyes were full of tears.

"Taladon's right," Tom whispered. "Silver is in good hands with the Mistress of the Beasts. I'm sure we'll see them again."

"But I can't just leave him there and forget about him!" Elenna protested. She stopped walking and caught hold of Tom's shoulder, forcing him to look at her. "What are we going to do?"

"We'll get Silver back. And Freya. I've lost my mother, remember. I'm not going to rest until we're all reunited."

"When?" Elenna insisted. "When will that happen?"

"Tom? Elenna?" called King Hugo.

He and Aduro were watching them from further down the stone corridor.

"Soon," Tom promised his friend as they began walking after the ruler of Avantia and his good wizard. "Do you think I'd let you down?"

But Tom had a feeling Malvel's games weren't over.

Win an exclusive
Beast Quest T-shirt and goody bag!

Tom has battled many fearsome Beasts and we want to know which one is your favourite! Send us a drawing or painting of your favourite Beast and tell us in 30 words why you think it's the best.

Each month we will select **three** winners to receive a Beast Quest T-shirt and goody bag!

Send your entry on a postcard to
BEAST QUEST COMPETITION
Orchard Books, 338 Euston Road, London NW1 3BH.

Australian readers should email:
childrens.books@hachette.com.au

New Zealand readers should write to:
Beast Quest Competition, 4 Whetu Place, Mairangi Bay,
Auckland NZ, or email: childrensbooks@hachette.co.nz

**Don't forget to include your name and address.
Only one entry per child.**

Good luck!

Join the Quest,
Join the Tribe

www.beastquest.co.uk

Have you checked out the Beast Quest website?
It's the place to go for games, downloads, activities,
sneak previews and lots of fun!

You can read all about your favourite Beasts, down-
load free screensavers and desktop wallpapers for
your computer, and even challenge your friends
to a Beast Tournament.

Sign up to the newsletter at www.beastquest.co.uk
to receive exclusive extra content and the oppor-
tunity to enter special members-only competitions.
We'll send you up-to-date info on all the Beast
Quest books, including the next exciting series
which features six brand-new Beasts!

Get 30% off all Beast Quest Books at www.beastquest.co.uk
Enter the code BEAST at the checkout.

Offer valid in UK and ROI, offer expires December 2013

All books priced at £4.99,
special bumper editions
priced at £5.99.

Orchard Books are available from all good bookshops, or
can be ordered from our website:
www.orchardbooks.co.uk,
or telephone 01235 827702, or fax 01235 8227703.

Series 7: THE LOST WORLD
COLLECT THEM ALL!

Can Tom save the chaotic land of Tavania from dark
Wizard Malvel's evil plans?

978 1 40830 729 8

978 1 40830 730 4

978 1 40830 731 1

978 1 40830 732 8

978 1 40830 733 5

978 1 40830 734 2

**Series 8: The Pirate King
COMING SOON!**

Balisk the Water Snake
Koron, Jaws of Death
Hecton the Body Snatcher
Torno the Hurricane Dragon
Kronus the Clawed Menace
Bloodboar the Buried Doom

Mortaxe the Skeleton
Warrior controls the good
Beasts of Avantia. Can
Tom rescue them before it
is too late?

978 1 40830 736 6